# The One That Got Away

BY
AMAZON BESTSELLING AUTHOR
## RUSS TOWNE

ISBN: 978-1-948245-30-2

Copyright © 2021 Russ Towne

Russ Towne Publishing
Campbell, California

Editing: Karen M. Smith, Hen House Publishing

# Table of Contents

# Chapter 1

# Bushwhackers

Asa Boyar crouched and peered over the boulder at the lone rider coming up the trail about five hundred yards away and said to his two companions, "This is gonna be easy."

Dabbs Daggett shooed away a fly and sneered, "It will be if you don't get cocky. Wait 'til he's so close you can't miss."

Boyar turned and stood facing him, towering over the other man, and snarled, "You wanna take the shot, smart-ass?"

Cord Grundman jumped in before fists started flying. "C'mon, Dabbs, you know Asa's a better shot than us."

Dabbs looked into the cold dark eyes that bore down on him, and backpedaled, "Yeah, but I was just remindin' him to be patient. One clean shot saves us from huntin' down a wounded man."

Asa held Dabbs' gaze and snarled, "You're just skeered you might hafta shoot it out with someone who knows you're there. Don't worry. I know what I'm doin'. Ain't I already proved it three times?"

Cord continued trying to assuage the tall man, "You sure did, and we got three horses, pistols, rifles, some money, and other good stuff for just the cost of three well-placed bullets. I'd call that a damn good deal."

Asa's lips curled, but his smile held no mirth as he turned to Cord, "You sure he still has his month's pay after the drive? That just don't seem right to me."

Cord, the shortest of the three, quickly nodded, "Yup. I watched him like a hawk. He only bought two drinks, a few supplies, and got a room—"

Asa interrupted, "For just hisself? No whores or nothin'?"

"Just hisself."

"No gamblin'?"

"Nope."

Dabbs spit in disgust and offered, "Must be a saint. What's the point of money if ya don't spend it on whores, booze, and gamblin'?"

Asa smiled, "That just leaves more for us." He pointed at the approaching rider and said, "Well, he's soon gonna be a dead saint. Let's stop yakkin' and get to work. My pecker's been itchin' for them whores in Jones Gulch."

On the trail below, Buck Evans cautiously scanned in all directions as he rode, a habit he'd picked up many years prior. It helped keep him alive. His sturdy bay had more heart than good looks, which was just the way Buck liked him. Buddy had never let Buck down. Death often came swiftly to men who rode unreliable mounts, a lesson many a rider of handsome but heartless horses learned the hard way.

The lone rider smiled at the thought of a month's pay in his saddlebag. Early on, Buck found that sometimes honest work could be scarce. He'd seen too many honest men become desperate from lack of work. Some turned to crime when their money and luck ran out. Buck wasn't the kind to blow a month's pay on a couple of bawdy nights in a saloon. Nor was he one of those who dreamed of someday owning a ranch. Buck didn't want to be tied down to any one place, no matter how beautiful it was. At least not yet anyway. There were still too many other things to see and experience.

Buck's strategy was as unique for a wrangler as it was audacious. He sought and found honest, hard-working, ambitious, intelligent people, with sound business ideas. He knew that a lot of crooks had all those same attributes—except, of course, honesty—and that hard-working, intelligent, ambitious crooks were some of the worst kind. They'd work harder and be more creative to take everything one owned. Buck learned the importance of being very careful about whom he trusted after having been so wrong about a man he'd made his deputy when he'd been Destiny's town marshal. That mistake led to ten years in prison for crimes he didn't commit and nearly cost him his life. The betrayal also led to the loss of his beautiful fiancée, Lacy—and good riddance. Buck soon learned he was far better off without her.

After those harsh lessons Buck first made certain of a person's honesty before considering investing along with them as their silent partner. Some of the businesses failed despite his partners' best efforts. Some did little more than survive. But many thrived beyond what anyone had expected.

He was often amazed and well rewarded by what could be accomplished when honest, hard-working, ambitious, and talented people were given sufficient funds to grow businesses with little or no debt, so they could survive and thrive through the inevitable tough times that often crippled or killed their heavily indebted, poorly funded, and not-as-well-managed competition.

Buck did not consider himself a wealthy man. No one who saw him in his worn work clothes with thickly calloused hands and sun-darkened, weathered skin would ever guess his financial situation. He never flaunted his money; it wasn't his style, nor was it wise to do so, especially as a loner. In fact, he rarely carried much money on him. His frugal lifestyle on the trail didn't require it. When he found a person and idea worthy of an investment, he simply wired requests for whatever amount he needed from any of more than a dozen partners and quickly received the funds.

A horse nickered not far away. Buddy's head jerked upward, ears pricked forward.

Asa Boyar saw the horse's reaction to their presence and knew the rider would likely be alerted. He raised his Winchester to draw a bead on his target.

Buck caught the glint of sunshine off the rifle's barrel as it swung. He ducked and spurred Buddy as a bullet ripped a searing, six-inch-long gash through the skin along the back of Buck's lowered left shoulder, knocking him from the saddle. He fell out of sight of the bushwhackers behind a large boulder and down a steep ravine.

Asa roared, "Got him! It's payday, boys!"

They ran to the spot where the rider was shot, but their smiles vanished when neither man nor beast was in sight.

Dabbs Daggett pointed at some crimson splashes on the trail and a blood smear that led over the lip of the ravine. "Damnit! Looks like he fell all the way down there."

Cord Grundman said, "Well if your shot didn't kill him, the fall surely did."

Asa asked, "You willin' to bet your life on that?"

The men cautiously peered over the edge. Cord asked, "Can ya see him? That's a long climb down."

Daggett suggested, "Mebbe we won't need to. Let's just find his horse and go. I reckon his pay'll be in his saddlebags along with the rest of his gear. And we'll get his rifle and tack off the horse."

Cord said, "Sounds good to me. If his pay's not in the bags, we can then go down and get it."

Daggett said, "And if he was only wounded, he'll have likely bled out by the time we have to go near him."

Asa spit and hissed in a derisive tone, "You boys got it all figured out, doncha? But you're forgettin' something. I saw him look my way just before I fired. If he's alive, he might get away and someday finger me as the shooter. I don't fancy wearin' a noose necktie."

Dabbs blurted, "But ..."

Asa snarled with a voice that was deep and menacing, "I'm goin' and you're comin' with me, hear?" He thought, *And if I get real lucky, the two of you will get shot, so I can keep everything for myself. Men like you to ride with are a dime a dozen.*

His accomplices shot each other a quick look, then turned to Asa and nodded.

Hopefully, Cord said, "His horse run off. We should get it before it gets too far away."

Asa shook his head, "We'll catch him later."

The bottom of the ravine was far enough down that they had to tie all three of their ropes end to end, anchored by a sturdy tree. They'd knotted it at appropriate intervals to make it easier to maintain a grip.

Asa threw down the secured rope and looked at the others. "What're ya waitin' for? Go down and get him!"

Dabbs objected, "But he could pick us off as we go down."

The tall man said, "I'll cover you from up here."

As Asa looked into the ravine, the others shot disgusted looks at him.

Sensing their frames of mind, he turned to them and asked, "Either of you got a problem with that?"

Their mutiny transformed into acquiescence in a heartbeat.

"I didn't think so." The tall man grabbed his Winchester, aimed it into the ravine, and demanded, "Get goin'!"

Cord drew a deep breath, eased over the edge, and began his descent. He jumped the last few feet, landed hard, and rolled, coming up in a crouch with his gun drawn, panting. He wiped the sweat from his eyes and looked around.

Dabbs yelled, "See him?"

"No, but I see where he landed and there's a blood trail. C'mon down. We'll flush him out if he's still alive. I'll help cover you."

When Dabbs reached the bottom and drew his pistol, he sighed with relief that he hadn't gotten a bullet in his back. He shouted, "Okay, Asa. Three can flush him out better than two. We'll cover you."

Asa muttered, "Gotta do everything myself." He laid the rifle against a boulder and headed down.

Buck Evans came to and felt a searing pain behind his left shoulder and running down his back. His vision blurred and he shook his head to clear it. It felt mule-kicked. Gingerly palpating his scalp with his fingertips, he felt a large bump and a trickle of blood drip from a small cut above his left temple.

Buck mentally traced his fall and realized he'd rolled down the wall of the ravine and bounced off a mound into a depression on the opposite side from where he'd been shot. Buck was amazed at his good fortune. *If I'd fallen straight down rather than rolling, I'd have likely died on impact; and, if I hadn't bounced into the depression, the bushwhackers would have seen and shot me from above.*

He thought about the bushwhackers. *How many are there? Please, let them leave me for dead.* The sound of the rope smacking against the ravine wall informed him that Lady Luck hadn't been so kind. *Guess that was askin' too much of the lady.*

He reached for his pistol, a six-shot Colt Army Model 1860 revolver that had been converted for metallic cartridges, hoping his fall hadn't ejected it from the holster. To his great relief, he found it where it was supposed to be. *The thong did its job.* Buck slipped the leather loop off the hammer, grateful not to be wounded on his shooting side. He listened, trying to focus his mind and vision through a thick veil of pain, sweat, and blood.

Two of the bushwhackers were close. Buck heard them breathing hard, their boots shuffling in place just on the other side of the mound. He heard a third man making his way down the ravine wall.

*Hopefully, the two already down here will stay crouched where they are and wait for the third before making a move.*

Buck tried to leap to his feet, but blood loss, pain, and dizziness made his effort more like a drunken stagger. Daggett and Grundman heard him and wheel toward him, guns blazing.

If he'd been standing upright, his head and chest would have been visible and an easy target. Daggett and Grundman's two slugs would have torn into him. Fortunately, the uneven ground beneath his feet made him fall forward against his side of the mound as the bullets whizzed above.

The two bushwhackers weren't so lucky. They were caught out in the open on the other side of the mound and equally easy targets only six feet away. Steadied by the mound, Buck fired at the shorter of the two attackers, hitting him in the chest and a little to the left of center. Cord Grundman collapsed, his lifeless face smacking into the rocky ground.

ᔕ•ᘓ

Dabbs panicked. He liked being a bushwhacker. There was little risk if the first bullet fired was into the back of a surprised victim. That usually ended things exactly the way Dabbs liked it. *I didn't sign up for no shoot-out!*

Dabbs panic-fired. His round smashed into the mound inches below Buck's face and threw debris into his eyes. Buck ducked, shook his head, blinked rapidly, and used the pinky of his gun hand to try to regain enough of his vision to be able to fend off his attacker. Instead of pressing his advantage and rushing his wounded quarry, Dabbs Daggett ducked behind the mound opposite where Buck laid, and waited, hoping Asa would hurry and come finish off their prey.

ᔕ•ᘓ

Asa Boyar was about three-quarters of the way down the rope when the firing began. Knowing he was a sitting target hanging from the rope, he panicked, let go, and jumped from too high up. His right foot glanced off a large rock on the bottom, and his left foot fell the remaining two feet to the ravine floor. Boyar screamed as his right ankle shattered.

Dabbs Daggett yelled, "You hit?"

Asa hissed through his pain, "No. Broke my ankle. Don't worry 'bout me. Get *him*!"

Dabbs said, "He got Cord."

"So what? There's still two of us and only one of him, and he's been shot." Asa crawled to Dabbs.

Daggett turned to him and whispered, "This one's not so easy to kill."

Asa snarled in a voice icier than a winter frost, "Time to put him below snakes."

Buck used their distraction to make his way leftward in a crouch to flank the bushwhackers. They'd have heard him if they hadn't been making so much noise.

Asa pointed the muzzle of his gun and made a motion indicating they should climb over the mound as he silently mouthed, "Let's jump him."

Daggett nodded, and they both moved into a position to spring. The taller man leaned forward, balanced on his good foot, giving Daggett room to leap; however, he held back just long enough to ensure Dabbs caught any bullets flung their way. Asa fully intended to use the man's body as a shield as he threw lead at their quarry.

Unfortunately for the tall bushwhacker, Buck was now on their side as he rounded the rise from their right and fired twice. Both slugs slammed into the right side of Asa's chest. He crumpled, his body shielding Daggett's as the latter scrambled over the top to the other side.

Asa gurgled bloody foam and fell silent.

Dabbs said, "Hey, mister."

"Yeah?"

"You're wounded and the walls of this ravine are too high and steep for you to get out of here on your own."

Buck considered the outlaw's message. *He's got a point. I've lost a lot of blood and can't reach the wound to try to staunch the bleeding. There's no way I can climb out of here with only one good arm. I'll bleed out if I stay down here by myself.*

Daggett continued, "I'm not hurt and could help you."

"How?"

"Well, I could climb the rope. When I reach the top, I could untie if from the tree, tie it to the saddle's pommel, and let my horse pull you up."

*It's likely he'll shoot me if he gets half the chance, but what hope do I have without him?*

The bushwhacker said, "Throw me your pistol and c'mon out. I won't shoot."

Buck hesitated, knowing that either way it was likely to be the last decision of his life. He tossed his pistol over the mound, about ten feet beyond where he guessed his attacker stood.

Daggett laughed and taunted, "You're a bigger fool than I thought!" He turned to fetch the pistol several feet behind him.

Buck shouted, "You forgot something!"

Daggett turned toward his victim as Buck grabbed the knife from the sheath sewn into the inside of his right boot and threw it into the chest of the last bushwhacker. He took even less pleasure in killing that man than he had when forced to kill the others.

*I just killed the one man who could've gotten me out of here. Not that I had much choice.*

Buck retrieved his gun, then reloaded, checked, and holstered it, putting the thong back securely over the hammer. He pulled his knife from the bushwhacker's body, wiped the blade on the dead man's pants, and sheathed it. Exhausted, he sat down to think, and probably to bleed out and die.

Not long after, he, too, fell face down into the dirt.

# Chapter 2

# Happiness and
# Heartbreak

Buck heard something trying to penetrate the nothing-ness of his unconsciousness. At first it seemed faint, indis-tinguishable. He focused on the sound.

*A woman. Shouting.*

*How much time has passed? No idea. Probably still the same day. Doubt if I'd have survived the night with how much blood I've lost.*

"Hey, mister! You alive?"

It took several seconds for Buck to summon his strength enough to respond through his parched throat. "Yes."

The young woman thought she heard something but couldn't be sure. She was about to shout again when she saw his head move.

"You hurt?"

He tried to shout louder but his voice reached her as barely a whisper. "Yes. Shot. Behind my left shoulder. Bushwhacked." He panted, trying to catch his breath. "Need water."

She ran to get a canteen, tied it to a rope, and lowered it as far as it would go. It was still about two-thirds from the bottom. The young woman aimed it so it would fall in what looked like a soft patch near the man and let go. It hit two feet from his left elbow and bounced into him. He winced and jerked his elbow to his side.

The woman shouted, "Sorry, mister."

Buck slowly sat up, teetering. He reached for the canteen, breathing hard, pulled the cork with his teeth, spat it out, and drank what to him seemed like the best-tasting water he'd ever had.

Buck said, "Don't be. If it had fallen much farther away, I might not have had the strength left to get it."

He drank again and felt a bit more of his strength return with every careful swallow. *Pace yourself. Don't want stomach cramps.*

She saw the three bodies lying around him and a shiver ran down her spine, thinking, *three horses were tied to a fallen tree near the trail when I rode up. Must have been the bushwhackers'. But how do I know the three dead men are the bushwhackers? Maybe their target and two of the bushwhackers are the dead ones. That seems as least as likely as their victim getting jumped but managing to kill all three and living to tell about it. What if the man I'm talking to is a bushwhacker and I free him? There's got to be a way to quickly figure out if he is one of the outlaws.*

She shouted down to him. "What's your name, mister?"

"Buck Evans."

"Hold on." She ran to the horse she'd rode in on, rummaged through a saddle bag and found a bill of sale with the name Buck Evans on it, and ran back to the lip of the ravine.

"I have your horse. He showed up at our house without a rider. I thought someone might have been thrown and needed help. Followed his tracks back to you."

"Mighty glad you did."

His head throbbed. *Dizzy. Won't be long before I lose consciousness.*

The woman called down, "Can you reach the rope and tie yourself to it?

Buck saw the end of it was only about fifteen feet away, but in his condition, he wasn't sure he could make it. He didn't waste energy answering her. He staggered to his feet and stumbled toward it. Buck fell, tried to stand, and fell again. *Lost too much blood.* Panting and bathed in sweat, he tucked his left arm near his chest to try to minimize the excruciating pain, then crawled three-limbed the rest of the way to the rope. He used the ravine's rocky wall to steady himself as he rose to his feet, then continued leaning against it as he tied the lifeline to himself.

Buck shouted, "I'm ready."

Out of sight, she shouted, "Hang on. Likely to be a rough ride."

Buddy grunted at the effort of lifting the nearly dead weight as the young woman coaxed him forward.

Buck felt himself slowly lifted off his feet. He crashed into the wall, tried to push off with his good arm and his legs, overcompensated, and spun around. His wounded shoulder smashed into a jagged outcrop. Buck gasped and ground his teeth from the pain.

*Much more of that and I'll be a corpse before I reach the top.*

He tried again to face the wall in a way that would help him avoid being dragged along its rough surface or bashed into it as he continued rising. With a little trial and more error, he discovered the right technique to keep him from spinning and bouncing too much.

The rope ground against the lip of the wall and dislodged debris that fell onto him.

She warned, "Don't look up."

With stones and dirt raining on top of his already-throbbing head, he thought, *No chance of that, lady.*

The trickiest part was when he reached the bottom of the lip, but with the woman's coaxing Buddy pulled him up and over. When she could see that the wounded man was safely on top, she halted the horse with a firm, "Whoa, boy!"

Buck tried to sit up and promptly fainted.

℘•℃

Buck opened his eyes to get his bearings. He was in a soft bed. The only light in the room was from the glow of an oil lantern. Beside him sat a young woman in a green gingham dress. Her features were slender, almost delicate. Reflections from the lantern's flame flickered in her eyes like glittering stars on a moonless night. Her long raven hair shimmered like moonlight dancing on a gentle river. The sight took his breath away. He had to look toward the ceiling to collect his thoughts.

"How'd I get here?"

"On a travois your horse pulled."

"You're a resourceful woman, Miss … uh …"

"Danbury."

"Thank you, Miss Danbury. You saved my life. How long have I been out?"

"Two days. You'd lost a lot of blood and had a high fever. We weren't sure you were going to make it, but the fever broke."

"We?" His breath caught as he awaited her reply and thought, *Please don't be married.*

She hesitated. *How much should I tell this stranger? I know nothing about him. He could still be a bad man, even if he wasn't one of the bushwhackers.* She studied his face. *probably mid-to-late thirties. Dark brown hair with a few flecks of silver. Ruggedly handsome. But that doesn't mean anything. I've heard tell that some of the most dangerous people are good-looking. There's a reason for the saying, "a wolf in sheep's clothes."* The young woman looked deeply into his steel blue eyes. The color reminded her of gun metal. *They seem to be forthright, without a hint of guile. If the eyes are truly a mirror into a person's soul, I can trust this man.*

"My grandmother and I."

Concern turned to relief at her words. He enjoyed look-ing at her. The young lady had an alluring combination of innocence balanced by an air of competence, confidence, and wisdom beyond her years. Her radiant smile seemed to magnify the lantern's glow and illuminate the whole room, yet she had a friendly, girl-next-door appeal that Buck much preferred to the distant, self-absorbed beauties who so often repelled him.

An awkward silence was finally broken when she began to answer unspoken questions.

"Mother died giving birth to me, Father of a heart attack six months later. Grandma said he really died of a broken heart. She was his mother. She took me in and raised me."

Buck said, "I'm sorry at your losses. It must have been a hard life for both of you."

She deflected the comment by saying, "Grandma's a strong and kind woman. She's been wonderful to me. Grand-pa had one of the largest spreads in the territory. Cattle and horses. When he got sick, he sold it all to buy us this house and banked the rest so that, if we were careful, we'd have enough to get by on."

A voice carried down the hall into the bedroom, "Maria, has Mr. Evans regained consciousness? I thought I heard a man's voice."

"Yes, Grandma."

A woman with gray eyes walked into the room as she pat-ted some stray strands of hair back into place. It was a tad lighter than the color of her eyes. She came over to the bed, looked at him, and smiled.

Maria said, "Mr. Evans, this is my grandma, Agnes Dan-bury."

Buck tried to rise, but Maria pressed both hands into his good shoulder and held him down with surprising strength for such a slender woman.

The older lady said, "Please, don't get up. It isn't neces-sary or even a good idea. You're a big man and if you fall, we might not be able to return you to bed."

She smiled, eyes twinkling.

He returned her smile and said, "I defer to your wisdom and kindness, ma'am."

"Please call me, Agnes. We're not much on formalities around here."

"Thank you, Agnes. You're welcome to call me, Buck."

"And you can call me, Maria," the young woman blurted with a bit more enthusiasm than she'd intended. She blushed. The other two exchanged glances and smiled.

Buck changed the subject. "I'm grateful for all that both of you did to keep me alive. I'll be getting on my way as soon as I can get on my feet. Sorry to be such a burden."

"Nonsense, young man! Far from being a burden, it's nice to hear a man's voice in our home. It's been a long time since my husband and son passed on. We don't get many visitors way out here, and I'm getting too old to go with Maria when she gets supplies in town."

She said it matter-of-factly, without a hint of self-pity in her voice.

"Well, ma'am, uh, Agnes, I appreciate your hospitality."

Her eyes twinkled again as she smiled broadly and joked, "Thank you for bringing some excitement into our lives."

"Anything to oblige, ma'am."

The three broke into laughter.

Two days later, Buck grew strong enough to stand. They helped him to the dinner table. His eyes grew wide at the offerings on the table as they helped him to his seat. Roast beef, mashed potatoes and gravy, green beans, homemade biscuits, butter, and honey. He'd been enticed for hours by the aromas as they cooked and wasn't disappointed by the sight.

"If all of this tastes as good as it looks and smells, I may eat you out of house and home."

Agnes said, "There's plenty where this came from, plus an apple pie's baking and should still be warm when it's time for dessert."

Buck shook his head in amazement and said with a laugh, "You two are spoiling me so much I may never want to leave!"

ℰ•℃

As sure as flowers bloomed in spring, Buck and Maria's affection toward each other grew greater every day. Agnes watched with mixed feelings. *They're clearly falling for each other. I like the young man. I believe he'd make a fine husband for Maria if he were ready to settle down. She'd be good for him, but he has the wanderlust in his eyes. He'll soon be moving along, and when he does, it's going to break her heart.*

When Buck healed well enough to help with the chores, he sharpened the axe, mended the gate, greased the wagon's wheels, fixed tools, and such. Maria made excuses to be with him as often as she could.

One morning when a thick, low mist blanketed the ground and Buck was out of earshot chopping wood, Agnes took Maria aside. They sat as the old woman looked into her innocent granddaughter's eyes. In a soft, kind, voice she said, "I believe that fine young man likes you very much, but he'll soon be moving on."

Maria paused and nodded. Tears forming in her eyes and her lower lip trembled as she spoke so quietly that her voice was little more than a whisper: "I can tell by the way he often looks off into the distance. But I love him, Grandma."

"I know, dear." She hesitated, weighing whether she ought to warn the level-headed but lovestruck young woman. If she did, she wondered if it would do any good. Agnes thought, *Probably not. It wouldn't have worked for me at her age, either.* Then she had a thought that made her grin, *Hell, if a good-looking man like that were interested in me, I wouldn't listen to the advice even at my age.* Her thoughts returned to Maria. *Still, I owe it to her to at least try.*

She reached out and squeezed the hand of a woman who not that long ago been a child and said in a loving voice with no hint of censure, "Be careful you don't do anything you'll come to regret later."

Maria gave her a woman-to-woman look that conveyed the message before her words did. "I won't, Grandma."

Buck completely healed but stayed to do more work around the house to repay his debt of gratitude to the ladies. That was what he told himself, anyway. It was true, and he'd have stayed even if he hadn't liked them so much. But it was only part of the truth. *Face it, you're also staying for their great cooking. But it's far more than that. I love being around them. And I can't take my mind off Maria. It's going to be mighty hard to leave that woman.*

Finally, the day came to tell them. At dinner that evening, he said, "Thank you for saving my life and treating me so well. It's been a real pleasure being here."

Maria's breath caught. She tried to speak but words failed her.

Agnes came to her rescue by saying, "Thank you for giving us such fine male company and for all the work you've done around here. It's been a real pleasure."

Maria regained her composure and, while looking down at her meal, asked softly, "When are you leaving?"

"At first light I reckon. I like being on the trail when the sun rises."

The women nodded.

Agnes said, "We'll fix breakfast for you and some grub to take on the trail."

"That's mighty kind of you but ..."

She winked and mock-scolded, "Listen to your elders, young man!"

He laughed and said, "Yes, ma'am!"

∞•∞

Agnes stifled a yawn and stretched. "I think I'll turn in. Dawn comes mighty early in these parts."

To Buck's surprise and disappointment, Maria said, "I guess I better turn in, too."

He'd hoped that could talk for a spell before getting some shuteye. With no one left to talk with, Buck soon headed for bed himself, but try as he might, he couldn't sleep. Thoughts of Maria swept away any chance of that. He stared at the dark ceiling and listened to a lone wolf's distant plaintive howl. *I know how you feel, wolf. I know how you feel.*

About an hour later, his door opened a crack and the soft glow from a lantern turned down low preceded the object of his thoughts and longings into the room. She held a slender finger to her lips and shut the door. The young woman hurried to his bed and set the lamp next to an unlit one on the bedstand.

"Maria, I ..."

"Shhh! Please, let me speak! I know you're going in the morning, no matter what. And I know it's wrong for me to be here now and to say what I'm about to say. I don't care! I love you and I think you like me, too. Even if we'll never see each other again after tomorrow, I want you to be the first man who makes love to me. It's a gift I can only give once, and I want to give it you. If I have that memory, I think I can bear the thought of you not being in my life."

Buck's heart leaped, but he hesitated. Despite his intense desire for her and due to his powerful love of her, he said, "Someday, you'll meet a man and want to marry him. You may wish you'd saved yourself for him. Many men aren't openminded about such things."

"Any man I marry will be kind and understanding."

"Maria, you are a dream come true. And I do love you. Very much."

He sat up in the bed and drew her to him. Their lips came together ...

They tried to remain as quiet as possible and mostly succeeded. They were quiet enough that, if the old woman had been asleep down the hall, she wouldn't have been awakened. But she wasn't asleep. Agnes knew the young man was too much of a gentleman to initiate anything and then leave her granddaughter with a broken heart, but she was equally certain that her granddaughter would visit him that night. She thought, *Because that's what I'd have done.*

The muted sounds coming from the room down the hall triggered a flood of memories of the first time she made love, despite the many decades that had gone by. Her reminiscences brought a wistful smile to her wizened face. Her thoughts gradually drifted back to the young woman down the hall. *Oh, Maria, you're too much like me. I hope your time with him is worth all the pain you're about to feel when your heart's broken.*

℘•℀

Five mostly breathless hours later, Maria reluctantly pulled herself from Buck's embrace whispering, "Grandma will soon waken. I must go back." Buck let her slip from his arms. It was one of the hardest things either of them had ever done.

Shortly later in the early morning hours, Agnes noticed the awkward glances and silence between the lovers as everyone prepared for Buck's departure. She made light conversation to help them cover for their feelings, but just once, she felt compelled to ask with an innocent look on her face, "Did you sleep well?"

Agnes laughed inwardly as they tried to hide their embarrassment. She chided herself. *Agnes, sometimes you're a wicked, wicked, woman.*

They finished breakfast. Buck packed his saddlebags, saddled Buddy, and turned to say the toughest goodbye of his life.

"Wait!" Maria shouted. She ran into her room and brought out a soft package wrapped in paper. She said, "This is for you, but you've got to promise that you won't open it until tomorrow morning."

He accepted the package with a puzzled look and teased, "Maybe just one peek?"

"Promise me!"

"I promise."

He carefully placed it into a saddle bag as Buddy stamped with impatience to get on their way.

Agnes hugged Buck and said, "I hate goodbyes. You take care, young man."

"Goodb—" his reply was cut short as she turned and hurried into the house.

Maria and Buck embraced and gave each other one last lingering kiss. She said, "Thank you, Buck. I'll never forget you."

Buck looked into her glistening eyes and said, "I'll never forget you either, Maria."

She slipped from his arms, turned, and walked back to the house. At the open doorway she again turned in his direction.

Buck mounted, and turned Buddy westward, and eased him into a trot.

Maria stood in the doorway, quietly sobbing, continuing to watch even as the tears blurred her vision of the man who held her heart as he rode out of sight and perhaps out of her life forever. Agnes came up behind and wrapped loving arms around the young woman's shoulders.

Still facing the direction Buck had gone, Maria said in a strong, confident voice, "It was worth it, Grandma, and I'll never, ever regret it."

Agnes, her own eyes moist, whispered, "I know, dear. I know."

They turned, stepped inside, and closed the door.

80 • CR

The next morning Buck woke after a long night with little sleep due to his memories of a certain young woman. He broke camp. As he prepared to mount up, he remembered the package and retrieved it. Buck ripped the paper and found a note attached to one of the four gifts. He read it and smiled for a long time. *Thank you, Maria! I hope our paths cross again someday.*

# Chapter 3

# Betrayal on the Trail

Two and a half years passed. Buck had often thought of the raven-haired, young woman. There had been other women since, but none made anywhere near the impression on his heart that Maria had.

Buck kept himself busy working at a variety of jobs, including riding shotgun on a stage line, as a wrangler and then as season foreman at a small ranch, and as temporary wagon master for a train that had lost their boss when a wagon crushed the original one during a particularly treacherous stretch of the journey. He moved on when each job was done and never took a long-term assignment. Buck found it a blessing that he could quickly learn new skills, but it was also a curse. The jobs he mastered soon bored him. Life was an adventure, and he planned to give it all he had in each role and then move on. Moving around also helped him to more quickly find good potential partners. During that time, he invested in a logging operation and a dry goods manufacturer.

Buck met a man in a sundry supply store who was trying to start up a freight hauling business. Buck's initial impression of Stan Woodling was favorable. He liked how he'd treated the supplier. Buck decided to apply for a job as a driver to help the man haul supplies to a mining camp about a week's journey away. It would give Buck more time to size up Stan Woodling. He could already see that the man was organized and handled people well without being a pushover. Buck thought, *He appears underfunded versus some of his competitors. His wagons are old but well-maintained. Stan Woodling clearly makes the most of what he has to work with. If I like what I see during the week, I'll offer to provide sufficient funding for more and newer wagons and better teams to pull them. But even more importantly, two of the other outfits I co-own would be happy to use a more reliable shipping service than their current haulers.*

Buck walked up to Stan Woodling and asked, "Looking for another driver?"

"Matter of fact, I am. Have any experience?"

"Six months as a wagon master for a train headed to California."

"Reckon that'll do, if you're willin' to take orders from me."

"Yessir, I am. I actually prefer not to be the boss. Don't need the headaches."

Woodling smiled ruefully. "I know what you mean. I guess I'm just a glutton for punishment, because leading men suits me fine. I'll be happy to take you on as a driver, but there's something you need to know first."

"What's that?"

"We've gotta go through country where two supply trains have been attacked in the last three months. One of the trains was large enough to fight 'em off, but the owner and three of the men on the smaller one weren't so lucky. They got killed defending the wagons. The other drivers were run off. My outfit is about the same size of the one that was lost. If you join us, we'll only be six men. I'd hire more if I could, but—"

"I understand. Thank you for your honesty, Mr. Woodling." Buck looked him in the eyes and said with conviction, "I don't go looking for fights, but I'll stand with you if one comes to us."

"Fair enough. Welcome aboard."

They shook on it with the grips and expressions of men whose words were far more reliable than others who tried to force their will with ironclad written contracts.

Buck said, "If you don't mind my asking, how well do you know the other four men? I reckon that, under the circumstances, it could be a mite tough to get a good crew."

Woodling nodded. "I know Thaddeus Pelton and Scott Rawlings quite well and trust them. They're good men who won't run from a fight. Don't know the other two hardly at all. Brass Rumpole is a big man who looks like he'd be handy in a tight spot. He recommended Rube Mulcahy. I offered Rube a job based on Rumpole's recommendation."

Buck nodded and said, "Thank you for the information."

ॐ•ॐ

The first night on the trail, when the boss was on lookout a little distance from camp, Brass Rumpole overheard Pelton and Rawlings laughing at a story the former had just told about how a hapless old wrangler named Henry had been thrown from his horse and found himself butt deep in a cactus. "He had so many needles stickin' out his rump, ol' Hen—"

Rumpole overheard the last sentence and mistakenly thought they were making fun of him and his last name. Brass went into a rage and flew into the two men with outstretched arms. The three crashed into Buck who'd just sat down to drink some coffee. The steaming liquid splashed into Buck's face as all four men sprawled in the dirt.

Buck got to his feet first and wiped his face with a sleeve in time to see Brass leap up and pull a knife on the other two men. Buck kicked Brass' hand and the knife went flying. Rumpole squealed in pain and rage as he wheeled on his assailant and threw a punch that would have knocked any man to the ground. But he'd telegraphed the move so clearly that Buck easily sidestepped it and had time to throw a quick jab into Brass' mouth and a powerful cross into his nose. Brass' nose gave way with a sickening crunch. Blood spewed from his flaring nostrils and dripped from split lips.

Stan Woodling rushed out of the darkness toward the commotion and shouted, "That's enough! What the hell started this?"

Brass spluttered, spewing blood into his boss' face and onto his clothes, and pointed at Pelton and Rawlings, "I was just teachin' these two a lesson 'bout what happens when someone makes fun of me or my name, when this other asshole—" he pointed at Buck "—jumped me when I wasn't lookin'!"

Rube shouted, "They ganged up on Brass."

Woodling turned to the other three and asked, "Was that the way of it?"

Rawlings answered, "No sir. Thad was just tellin' me a story about a cowpuncher who fell butt-first onto a cactus—"

Pelton added, "Yessir. My story had nothin' to do with Brass."

Buck added, "And Brass left out an important detail: he drew a knife on them. We're already short-handed, and I reckoned we need to keep all our drivers in one piece, so I kicked the knife out of his hand. Brass didn't take kindly to that and came after me."

Woodling looked at the bloody face of the much larger man and thought, *I'll bet he thinks twice before tryin' that again.* The boss then looked at his whole crew and said in a voice that trucked no argument, "I'm only gonna say this once. The next man who starts something is gonna find himself pullin' iron against me. Is that clear?"

Buck looked at the other men. *They don't appear to have a clue as to whether Woodling's bluffing, or how fast or accurate on the draw he might be, and they don't seem to be in a particular hurry to find out.* He smiled inwardly, his already high view of Stan Woodling going up a few more notches.

The next two days were long, hot, dusty, and hard, but otherwise uneventful. Woodling and the others found Buck to be a quiet, almost laconic, man who never shirked his duty and often did more than his share of even the dirtiest work. He was amiable, but largely kept to himself. The loner was observant and could be counted on, but he preferred to be left to his own private thoughts. Out of respect, they left him alone. Brass and Rube avoided him. Even Woodling found no need to tell Buck what to do. The man anticipated what needed to be done and did it before Stan needed to make the request.

Woodling thought, *Rawlings and Pelton are good men and I'm glad I have them, but Buck Evans is in a class by himself. He almost acts as though he was the one who owned the company, but in a humble and respectful way.* Woodling took another large mouthful of savory rabbit stew and thought, *Hell, he even volunteered to be our trail cook, and I'll be dogged if this isn't the best trail chow I've ever had.*

One thing about Buck did disappoint him, though: *There's no way he's gonna stay on as a driver long-term, but I'll take what I can get.*

Woodling looked at Rumpole and Pelton and frowned. *Unfortunately, I'm also stuck with them. Rumpole's a surly bully and Mulcahey's his lazy sidekick. Don't trust either of 'em as far as I can throw 'em. I'll breathe a whole lot easier when I can cut 'em loose after this shipment is delivered. It'll be good riddance.*

On the third day, the drivers' wagons were still in the same position they'd been the whole trip: Woodling led, followed by Buck Evans, then Pelton, Rawlings, Rumpole, and Mulcahy. Woodling was part-way around a bend in the road when he reined in and held up his arm to signal the others to stop. The others couldn't see why he'd halted. They set their brakes and climbed down to check on what the holdup was.

Buck thought, *Something's not right. This place is too convenient for an ambush.* He slipped his hammer thong, crouched a bit, and walked toward his boss while cutting an angle that brought him closer to a boulder and large tree. *If lead starts flying, I want to have cover close by.*

Being immediately behind the lead wagon in line he was the first of the dismounted drivers to get around the bend. A large tree lay across the road. He looked toward the thicker end of it and knew before he saw it what he would see. *Freshly cut.* He started to shout a warning when two shots rang out behind him. He cleared leather and pointed to the boulder and tree he'd picked out. Woodling nodded, pistol in hand, veering closer to the cover on the way to discover the source of the shots. Rawlings staggered around the corner, blood pouring from his right thigh. He gasped, "Rumpole shot Pelton in the back of the head, and Rube shot me. Thad's dead."

Buck ran to the wounded man and saw the traitorous drivers as they started around the bend toward them. Buck snapped off two quick rounds to discourage that behavior and, to his surprise, got lucky with one of his rounds winging Rumpole. Brass yelped as he and Rube scurried back around the curve and out of sight. Buck Evans helped Rawlings limp behind the boulder. Woodling reached the adjoining tree as several riders raced down a hill behind them, not more than two hundred yards away.

Buck shouted, "We're gonna get caught in a crossfire with the riders on one side of our cover and Brass and Rube on the other."

Stan nodded grimly. He said to Rawlings with a calmness he didn't feel, "The bullet went through and out, so there are two holes to plug. Gimme your handkerchief and neckerchief." The wounded man did as he was told. Woodling placed his and Rawling's handkerchiefs over the holes and used their neckerchiefs to tie them in place.

Buck replaced the two spent rounds in his .44 and whispered, "Gonna try to drop Rumpole and Mulcahy before the riders reach us, so we'll have some cover without those bastards sneakin' up behind us."

His boss nodded again.

Buck asked Rawlings, "Can you keep the curve in the road covered so Brass and Rube can't come at you that way while I go after them?"

Rawlings said through gritted teeth caused by the pain, "Yeah. Those bastards aren't gonna surprise me a second time."

Buck nodded and to his friends' surprise, raced uphill toward the riders. The horsemen fired some wild shots in his direction. Woodling asked aloud, "What's he doin'?"

Buck answered him by making a sharp turn to the right, running about fifty feet, and arcing back to get behind the traitors. He burst down the hill onto the road not twenty feet behind them. Gun in hand, Rube faced the curve from where he expected danger to appear. Brass had holstered his pistol to tend to the bullet hole in his powerful bicep. Though both had their backs to Buck, they heard the danger and whirled around. Rube nearly completed his arc when Buck's shot shattered his sternum. His hands clawed at the bloody hole, but his scream died before it left his mouth when his heart gave out.

Brass used Rube's body as a shield while he brought his .45 around. Buck fired once, hitting Rube's lifeless body, but the slug impacted at such a close range that the corpse began to slip from the grasp of the big man's wounded arm. The shift exposed one of Brass' legs. Buck fired at the exposed thigh a split second before Brass aimed for Buck's head and squeezed the trigger. Buck's slug crashed into the huge man's leg like a bolt of lightning, which caused the muzzle of the outlaw's pistol to drop enough to send the bullet drilling a hole through the cloth of Buck's shirt nearly centered in the area between his chest, arm, and armpit, missing all three.

Rumpole landed hard on his rump with Rube's carcass sprawled across his lap. Now his head and neck were exposed above the corpse. Buck took the shot that was available to him, aiming for the big man's head, but Brass was jerking around so much that the bullet landed low and nicked an artery in his neck. That would have ended the fight of ordinary men, but Brass shoved the dead weight off of him and raised his .45 to fire again. Buck closed the gap between them and drilled a hole between the outlaw's eyes. Brass toppled backwards, lifeless.

Before Buck could catch his breath and reload, four riders raced onto the road, whooping and hollering. They saw Buck and wheeled around to throw lead at him as he flung himself under a heavily laden wagon. Bullets slammed into the dirt inches from him as he scrambled out of their reach.

Two riders remained on the side of the wagon that faced the hill. The other two were trying to get around the panicked mule teams still harnessed to the wagons. If they could get behind the man under the wagon, he'd be boxed in and easy to kill in the crossfire.

Unfortunately for the riders, the wagons were parked so closely together that the mules' muzzles were only about three feet from the wagon in front of them. The spacing kept the train from getting too strung out and made it easier to defend while allowing the drivers to walk through the space when the mules were calm.

But the beasts were anything but calm now. The panicking teams snorted, screamed, and kicked, with teeth bared and nostrils flared. The two riders tried to force their mounts through the tight spaces, but their horses weren't having it. They reared and bucked at the danger.

The bottom of the wagon was low enough to make shooting him difficult while mounted. Buck knew they'd soon dismount and come at him from all sides. He crawled out the side facing away from the hill and saw the two riders who were trying to flank him. They were so busy trying to get their horses under control that it took a little time for them to see the man who crouched behind the wagon and fired at them at close range. Buck's shot slammed into his target's chest, knocking him from his horse. He aimed at the second rider and pulled the trigger. *Click!* Seeing the muzzle of the pistol pointed at him caused the man to jerk hard on the reins. His mount reared and bucked, tossing him under the hooves of two panicked mules. Buck could tell by the sounds that the outlaw would never be a threat to anyone again.

By then, the two other riders had dismounted.

One of the thieves shouted to his accomplice, "His gun's empty! Let's rush him before he can reload!"

Buck crouched, momentarily out of sight, as the outlaws rounded the back corner of the wagon just in time to each catch a tiny round in the chest from a derringer Buck produced from a hidden shirt pocket just below his belt. He was so close to them that he couldn't miss their hearts with both rounds. They dropped in their tracks.

Stan Woodling raced around the bend and was relieved to see his man standing. "We heard someone shout that your gun was empty. I came runnin' but heard the shooting immediately afterwards and figured you were a goner."

Buck held up a derringer with smoke curling from both barrels. "I'm still here, thanks to some gifts a special young woman gave me years ago."

Stan laughed and said, "Thank God for special young ladies." He saw the four dead bodies and whistled appreciatively at the number of men Buck had had to fight alone.

Buck asked, "What happened on your side?"

"Three riders came at us. From our cover Rawlings and I each plugged one and the third one musta decided it was too hot in the kitchen, 'cuz he turned tail and went for lookin' for his momma!"

They laughed.

"How's Rawlings?"

"Lost a lot of blood, but I think he's gonna make it."

They calmed and unhitched the teams, watered them, and picketed them in an area that allowed them to graze.

The men circled up and Rawlings asked, "Now what boss?"

"Don't rightly know. We've got six wagons but only three drivers, and you're wounded. The wagons are already fully loaded. We can't add weight to them without likely busting an axel or wheel."

Rawlings suggested, "We could try to hide three of the wagons, drive the other three to the mining camp, and come back for the last three."

Stan Woodling said, "If we do that, the odds are high that last three won't be there when we get back."

Buck said, "True, but we could hide five of the wagons while two of us could stay to guard them. The first one could take the sixth wagon to the mining camp and ask for men to come and help us drive in the rest. The eight-day roundtrip would also give Rawlings' leg a lot more time to heal."

Woodling thought for a moment and said, "That may be our best shot at getting all six wagons safely to the mining camp."

Buck offered, "If you'd like, I'd be willing to take the first wagon in so you could stay to tend to your wounded man and watch over your property."

Stan said, "Sounds like a plan. Thank you, Buck."

They spent the rest of the day hiding the wagons in a thicket of trees and tall bushes close to water. The men circled five of the wagons and the teams, picketing them within reach of water and adequate grazing. Buck and Stan then tried covering their tracks and camouflaging the wagons as best they could.

# Chapter 4

# Unhappy Customer

Buck was on the road at first light the next morning.

The next four days proved uneventful and gave him a lot of time to think. He often thought about Maria. He also occasionally thought of other women. One of those whose memories made him smile was Maisie Montrose.* She was a feisty, pretty girl who'd had a crush on him. Maisie's feelings changed when Buck escorted her to Mexico. She met and fell in love with a handsome hidalgo who was closer to her own age. She soon married the man. Buck harbored no hard feelings and he sincerely wished the newlyweds well.

He pulled into the mining camp about two hours before sunset. An off-shift group of about fifty curious miners came over to greet him.

A few minutes later, a cigar-chomping, fat fellow waddled out. The crowd of miners parted in his wide wake. He had an officious air about him that made Buck want to spit in disgust, but he held his phlegm, for the moment anyway.

---

* Read about Buck Evans and Maisie Montrose in "The Escort," published in *Six Shots Each Gun: 12 Tales of the Old West by Russ Towne* and Holly Bargo. Available on Amazon: https://www.amazon.com/Six-Shots-Each-Gun-Tales/dp/1796651532.

The dislikable fellow demanded, 'Where are the other wagons? There's supposed to be six!"

Buck looked him up and down from head to foot and back again without saying a word. He watched the man's indignation turn to rage and waited until the head man's jaw quivered until it became clear the cigar chomper was about to let loose with a stream of words Buck didn't feel in the mood to hear.

Buck said, "Why don't you ask the eight men who died when we were attacked?"

That news jarred the rotund man and the crowd of miners. The former's mouth moved, but he was momentarily at a loss for words. Buck felt no need to mention that the eight men who died had all been outlaws. That news could wait until later.

Buck continued, knowing full well that he was speaking to the camp boss, "And who are you? I want to speak to the person in charge."

The short man puffed himself up, thrust his chest out, spread his legs wide, and placed pudgy fists against what would have been his waist if it hadn't been so covered in blubber. "I'm Norval T. Krebs, the superintendent of this here mining operation."

Buck laughed. "No, really, who's in charge?"

Krebs' bulbous face became beet red as the miners nervously laughed.

Buck chided himself, *Okay, you had your fun with this oaf. It's time to get down to business.* "Oh, I see I made a mistake. You really are the one in charge. Excuse me, *sir.* Here is the first of your six wagons of supplies with Mr. Woodling's compliments, sir."

Krebs said, "Correction. Here is my *one* wagon of supplies. The other five wagons and what's inside them remain the property of Stan Woodling until they are in this camp. Where are they?"

"They are safe, four days' ride from here and guarded by Mr. Woodling himself and the only other survivor of our train."

Krebs waved his hand dismissively. "I ordered *six* wagons of supplies. They were all supposed to have arrived by tomorrow."

"If you say so, sir. I'm merely a driver."

"Well, how are you going to get the other five wagons here?"

"We were hoping, sir, that you could spare a few men for the eight-day round trip to help us drive them here."

Krebs shook his head and said, "That's out of the question! We need every man doing this job right here to stay on schedule."

"Well, that's a shame, sir. I guess Mr. Woodling will just have to take his five wagons of supplies somewhere else that can spare the men to help drive them in."

Krebs sounded shocked. His bullying tactics with mere vendors had always worked before. "B-but we need those supplies! They're *our* supplies!"

Buck said, "Well, I thought you needed them, too. What with winter storms coming, there's not enough time to order them from someone else for delivery before the first heavy snowfall. And you just said yourself that, until they reach this camp, the other five wagons of supplies still belong to Mr. Woodling. As it is, one of the mining camps I passed on the way here offered to supply the extra drivers we need, buy the supplies, and add fifteen percent to the price you offered."

Krebs face contorted so badly that Buck thought the man suffer from apoplexy.

The driver chided, "No need to get your knickers in a knot, sir. I turned down their offer. Mr. Woodling's an honorable man who believes a deal is a deal, so I knew he'd want to honor your agreement. But now that you said we don't really have a deal after all—"

"That's not what I said!"

"Well, then, what are you saying, Mr. Krebs?"

Buck looked at the amused looks on the miners' faces. They were clearly enjoying watching Krebs squirm.

Norval T. Krebs' mind raced to find a way to save face, get all the supplies, and somehow get something extra out of it for himself without the owners finding out. "Well, maybe I can let you have three men if the cost of their wages is deducted from the bill and Woodling knocks ten percent off the total."

"You do realize your counteroffer opens up the opportunity for other bidders, such as the other mining camps, right?"

Buck saw Krebs waver and knew he was close to breaking, so he worked a hunch. "Don't forget the six cases of whiskey that are sitting in one of those other five wagons."

Krebs blanched and the loner knew he'd struck a nerve with a correct guess. The murmuring of miners grew substantially louder when they heard the word whiskey. Buck thought, *Scamper juice has a way of doing that, especially to lonely miners who'd gone too long dry.* Buck had seen a separate bill of sale for the booze made out to Krebs rather than the name of the mining company as all the rest had been, but no shipping cost was added for the booze. *I knew it! Krebs slipped in the booze, so his employer would end up paying the freight charges, and then the low-life sumbitch planned to sell it at exorbitant prices to the miners and keep all the profits for himself. He's lower than a snake's belly! Well, let's see if I can make this snake pay in a way that will most hurt him.*

He said loudly enough so that every miner could hear, "I'm sorry for spoiling your surprise, Mr. Krebs. I saw the separate bill of sale made out just to your name for the booze. I planned to suggest that Mr. Woodling ask your company about it in case it was an error, but then I realized that you were going to give it to the miners as a bonus for the good job they're doing. Right?"

Krebs saw the trap that Buck had set. Now, if he tried to withhold or charge the miners for the scamper juice, he risked a strike and maybe a bloody mutiny. The oily man wore a forced smile and said, "Why, of course, that's exactly what I had in mind!"

The miners cheered and threw their hats in the air.

Buck said, "Well, since you're being so generous and supplying three men of my choosing at no cost to Mr. Woodling and you will pay the full price you agreed to pay, I guess we can throw in a credit for half the cost of the booze.

Krebs appeared punch struck. The expression on face was almost pitiful. He hadn't agreed to some of what Buck had just mentioned but knew it wouldn't be long under such a barrage from his tormentor before he did, so to avoid further pain and embarrassment, he said, "Okay! Okay! I agree to everything you just said. Now pick three volunteers and be on your way."

Buck said, "I'll do that as soon as you pay for the first wagon of supplies. The bill says cash on delivery."

Krebs sighed. "First, I have to get this wagon unloaded and the supplies inventoried, and then you'll get a company check."

Buck said, "Fair 'nough."

The boss man then shouted to a big man, "Sullivan, get some men to unload and inventory the supplies, then stow and secure it and report what's here to me."

"Yessir." Sullivan pointed at a half dozen men and said, "You just volunteered to unload this here wagon. Get to it."

Grumbling, they did as they were told.

Krebs wiped his sweat-soaked, balding pate with a handkerchief, turned his back on his antagonist, and waddled out of sight.

Buck smiled at the boisterous crowd of miners, and shouted, "Who wants to volunteer to go get the booze, er, five wagons of supplies?"

They all raised their hands and cheered.

# Chapter 5

# One More is Born

Buck returned with the miners who brought their bedrolls and a few personal supplies in the otherwise empty wagon. They smelled dinner cooking as they neared Woodling's camp. Stan greeted them with a "Howdy, boys! Hope you brought your appetites, because we cooked enough food for a dozen men."

The miners cheered.

After dinner, Stan took Buck aside and said, "Based on the way the miners were talking about what happened in the mining camp, it appears you may have a mighty interesting story to tell."

Buck smiled and said, "Well boss, let's just say you're unlikely to have that camp superintendent as a repeat customer."

"Oh, yeah? What happened?"

Buck described how the fat fellow had acted when he walked out to meet the wagon, then added, "He was so officious, it just raised my hackles. I didn't help things when I kept poking the snake." The loner went on to describe the conversation, frequently interrupted by his boss's laughter. Halfway through the tale, Woodling was guffawing so hard that he snorted and held up his hand to signal Buck to wait a moment to let him catch his breath.

When Buck finished his story, Woodling had laughed so hard he had to wipe tears from his eyes.

Stan joked, "After the way you behaved, I don't know whether to fire or promote you, but it sure sounds like that SOB got what he deserved. Now that I know the kind of snake he is, I wouldn't do business with him again if he begged me to."

They laughed again.

Then Buck became serious and said, "I didn't have your permission to offer to pay for half the booze. You're welcome to subtract the cost of that from my pay."

Woodling laughed again. "Thank you for your offer, but that won't be necessary. You kept him from chiseling me several different ways that would have cost me a lot more, and, besides, the laughs I got from your story were well worth the price of half the scamper juice!"

"Thanks, boss. Also, on the way over here, the miners asked me what kind of man you are. I told them the shape of your shadow and that you were a solid man. They asked if you might have openings as drivers for them. I knew you would never recruit a customer's men, but since they were the ones who brought the subject up, I said I'd check with you."

Woodling picked up a stick, pulled out a pocketknife, opened the blade, began whittling, and said, "You've been with them for four days. I'll bet you have a pretty good measure of each man by now. What do you think of them?"

"Well, first off, I picked each man because I liked the cut of his jib. Then we all took turns driving the wagon, caring for the team, and setting up and breaking camp. I believe they'd all be good men and drivers. As an added bonus, although they were careful not to badmouth Krebs, they clearly detest the man about as much as I do. And they're sick to death of mining."

"Those are all good reasons to hire them, but I've got one more."

"What's that?"

Stan said, "Once we deliver the supplies in the other five wagons, we'll have six empty wagons to get back home, but only three men to do it unless we hire the miners on."

Buck gave his boss a knowing smile and said, "That thought had crossed my mind."

"I figured it had. You're always thinking ahead."

They laughed again.

Buck stood to stretch his back and arms, then sat down and said with a groan, "After eight days in that wagon, my back isn't quite as young as it used to be."

Stan said, "True, and we get to do it all over again starting tomorrow. Hey, how much do you want to bet that Krebs will hide when we arrive and make some underling deal with us?

Buck chuckled and said, "I'll bet you're right!"

They sat in the comfortable silence of good friends. Buck plucked a blade of grass and chewed an end of it while Stan whittled.

The loner asked, "How did it go while we were gone?"

"We didn't encounter any more varmints of the two-legged variety but did have to scare off a bear who got a little too interested in the food in the wagons."

Buck grunted at the thought.

Stan continued, "We buried the dead men after collecting everything of value they had, except their clothes. They certainly didn't need their stuff anymore. I'll sell everything I can when we get back to town."

The loner nodded, but felt a twinge of something he couldn't quite place, and thought to himself, *What am I feeling about Stan's plans?* Then it occurred to him: *Disappointment. About what? Not getting a share of the dead men's things? No, of course not! I don't want blood money. No, I'm disappointment in Stan. But why? What was he supposed to do with the valuable items? Leave them to decay in the weather? Who would it hurt if Stan sells the stuff and keeps the money for himself? No one.*

Woodling noticed the vaguely troubled look on his friend's face, guessed the reason why, and corrected Buck's misconception by adding, "In addition to Thad's full pay, I plan to give all the proceeds to Thad Pelton's widow. The poor woman's got two young kids. She's going to need every penny to get by on. I'm also going to make certain that she and the kids always have a roof over their heads and never go hungry."

Buck scolded himself for ever doubting the man's intentions, and said, "That's a mighty fine thing for you to do. I'd be proud to float my stick alongside yours anytime."

"Thank you, Buck. I feel the same way about you."

"I'm glad to hear that Stan, because I have an offer for you."

Woodling looked up from his whittling with a surprised expression on his face.

Buck continued, "I'd like to invest in your company as a silent partner. I can supply a substantial amount of funding to allow your business to grow more quickly, get new wagons and more of them, the teams to pull them, drivers to dive them, warehouses, and whatever else you'll need. I also know some companies that require your services and could begin sending work your way as soon as you're able to take it on." Buck paused to give Woodling a chance to digest what he was saying, then asked, "You interested in hearing more?"

Stan smiled and said, "I *knew* you weren't just some driver! Hell, you've already helped save my company and my life. I wouldn't be here if you'd allowed the four riders to flank Rawlings and me when we were dealing with the other three. You've acted like an unofficial silent partner all along—and a damn good one at that! Might as well make it official. I'd be proud to go into business with you. What, specifically, do you have in mind?"

Fifteen minutes of working out the details later, they shook on it and another partnership was born.

80•03

They were hours from town and giving the teams a break at a watering hole when Stan walked over to Buck, who was staying to himself as usual, and asked, "Well, partner, what do you plan to do once you draw your pay for this job?"

"I've been doing some thinking on that. I'll arrange to have the money wired to you for the business expansion, then I think I'll mosey over to thank that special young woman who gave me those gifts that kept me alive when we got jumped. Her house is only about two days' ride away."

Stan smirked and winked, "Right in the neighborhood. How convenient."

# Chapter 6

# Surprise Reunion

The maelstrom of conflicting thoughts and emotions crashing around inside Buck's head all morning and most of the prior night continued unabated as he rode toward Maria's and Agnes' home. *Will Maria want to see me after all this time? Does she hate me? Will she even remember me? Will my visit reopen a painful wound? Is it fair to show up unannounced? Do they still live in the same house? Has she stayed the same? Of course, she's changed! She was a young woman with her whole life ahead of her. How could she not have changed? I wonder what's different and what's stayed the same? I sure hope Agnes is okay. I sure like that old lady. Did she know what Maria and I did the night before I left? How could she not know? Maria and I were so flushed with love that a blind woman in a dark cave would have known! And Agnes was far from blind.* To Buck's surprise, he blushed like a schoolboy at the thought of her knowing.

He nearly turned around twice, but curiosity compelled him to keep going. The only way he'd ever know the answers was to see her. He'd often thought of Maria, sometimes for days on end. *Why didn't you just up and marry the girl?* But he knew why. He hadn't been ready. It would have been a mistake. But it had often felt like a mistake not to have married her, especially on cold and lonely nights and days. Buck asked himself, *Are you ready now?* The thought excited and worried him. *What happens if I am? What would she say? But what if I'm not? I guess I'll have to spend some time with her to know.*

Buck crested a hill and saw their house in the distance. His heart beat so hard and fast he has to force his breathing to slow down. *My hands are clammy. That woman sure has a hold on me even after all this time.*

As Buddy bought him nearer, Buck noticed her sitting on a porch swing holding something in her arms.

As he neared, she rose, and exclaimed, "Is it really you, Buck Evans, after all these years?"

Buck removed his hat and said, "Hello, Maria. I'm mighty happy to see you."

Maria smiled and said, "Haul off and cool your saddle. The watering trough and pump, and saddle tree are still around back for Buddy." She walked down the porch steps to pet his mount, shifted what she was carrying so it lay across one arm, and used her other arm to pat Buddy's neck. She smiled and talked to the horse. "How are you, old friend? Been a good boy?"

Buddy nickered at the attention.

Maria asked, "I wonder if he remembers me."

Buck looked at her and said, "You're unforgettable Maria."

She looked at Buddy a moment, thinking of earlier times, and said in a soft voice, "So are both of you."

Buck glanced at what she'd been carrying just as it gurgled and moved.

Maria noticed his gaze and said, "Buck, meet my little one." She looked at the loner to watch his reaction when she said, "His name is Buck. He's three months old and looks just like his father."

Buck's first rection was panic, but logic caught up with him as he thought, *I can't be the father! It's been far too long since we were together.* Relief washed over him soon followed by sadness for what might have been.

Buck looked more closely at the baby and realized the little guy looked nothing like him. He had a shock of red hair, freckles, and green eyes.

Maria enjoyed watching Buck's various expressions as he studied the baby. After several moments, she said, "You're welcome to tend to Buddy around back. I'll bring out some lemonade. We can drink it on the porch while we wait for my husband to come home for lunch.

The word "husband" hit him like a bolt of lightning, down deep. He tried not to react, but Maria couldn't help but notice.

Buck said, "Yes, I'll tend to Buddy." He thought as he led the horse around back, *Get hold of yourself! Of course, a great woman like Maria is married. She couldn't wait forever to see if you were ever going to be ready to get hitched. She's beautiful, attractive ten different ways, fun, intelligent, and a wonderful woman to boot. Any man in his right mind would jump at the chance to have her. What's that say about you? She was yours for the taking and you let her get away.*

Buck took care of Buddy and left him tied under a shade tree near the water trough. He walked back around to the front and climbed the porch steps. She handed a glass of lemonade to him as she suggested a chair that she'd placed across from the porch swing.

As he sat, he said, "Thank you. How's Agnes?"

A shadow darkened Maria's face. "My grandma died about eight months ago. She never got to see the baby."

"I'm terribly sorry to hear that. I really liked her."

"Thank you. I miss her terribly. At least she died in her sleep. She—oh, look, here comes my husband now."

Buck stood as a tall, well-built man climbed the steps, saw the visitor, stopped, and extended his hand.

Buck shook it as Maria said, "Jake, this is Buck Evans, an old friend of my grandma's and me." Jake paused for an instant when he heard the name Buck, then gave their guest a warm smile as he said, "Hello and welcome!"

Maria continued the introductions, "Buck, this is my husband, Jake Duncan."

The two men sized each other up out of curiosity rather than wariness. Buck noticed Jake's red hair and the freckles and green eyes on his friendly face. His skin was bronzed from working in the sun, and his hands showed the callouses of a working man.

Buck observed to himself, *Many husbands in this situation would be threatened or try in various ways to mark their territory, but Jake seems genuinely friendly and curious, not intimidated at all.*

Maria walked up to her husband and kissed him on the cheek. "Your lunch is warming on the stove. Beef stew."

Jake smiled and said, "Thank you, dear." He turned to Buck and said, "Please join us for lunch. Maria's a great cook and always makes more than enough."

Buck hesitated, "I don't mean to intrude."

Maria said, "Jake's right, there's plenty, and we have a lot of catching up to do. It's been what, three years?"

The meal was as delicious as advertised, and there was still quite a bit left after all had eaten their fill. The baby cried shortly after the end of the meal, and Maria excused herself to go feed him.

Jake suggested, "Let's sit out on the porch. It's cooler there."

When they were seated, Duncan asked, "So how did you, Maria, and Agnes meet?"

Buck told him the story of the bushwhackers and how Maria found and rescued him. He said, "She is quite a woman! She saved my life."

Jake smiled, the deep love he felt for her evident on his face. "She never mentioned that. Maria told me she wanted to name our baby Buck after a man who had helped Agnes and her for a month and wouldn't accept a dime the whole time. It is good to finally meet our baby's namesake."

Buck continued, "Actually, that wasn't the only time Maria saved my life. She did it again only a couple of weeks ago."

Jake's jaw dropped and he began to ask, "How—"

Maria walked in with a cooing baby, and asked, "Did I hear you say I saved your life recently? How? We haven't seen each other in years."

Buck told them about the train of freight wagons getting attacked and how he'd run out of ammo in his gun and didn't have time to reload when the last two riders came up to finish him off. He paused to let his predicament sink in, then smiled and pulled the front of his shirt out of pants, pointing at the pockets that had been hidden beneath his belt. "Remember these?

Maria smiled. "It's one of the shirts I sewed for you."

Buck pulled out the derringer. "And this?"

"My grandfather's derringer!"

"The shirt kept it out of sight until I needed it, but it sure came in handy when I did. Thank you, Maria, for saving my life a second time!"

She said, "I just copied an idea my grandma came up with to keep Grandpa's derringer out of sight, but handy in case he ever needed it."

Jake laughed, pulled up the front of his shirt and showed Buck the two hidden below-belt pockets in it. He said as he pulled out a derringer that looked identical to the one Buck held, "The tradition lives on!"

Maria said to Jake, "I wanted you to have one just like Grandpa's and found it at a gun store."

Buck saw the way they looked at each other and thought, *They share the rarest and most precious kind of love, one untainted by possessiveness, jealousy, or doubt.* He felt happy for them and with the joy came the realization that Maria and he also shared that kind of love, years ago, and still today. It lived on and never died. That thought brought a smile to his face.

Jake looked at his pocket watch and said, "Oh, I better get back to work. I've enjoyed our time together, Buck. Please stay as long as you'd like. It sounds like you and Maria have a lot of catching up to do." He shook hands with their guest, kissed his wife and baby, and left.

Buck observed, "I can see that he's a good man, one I'd be proud to call a friend, and that you are very happy together."

Maria smiled and looked at him. "I was blessed to find two such men: one a dear friend forever and the other a dear husband."

They were silent for a time, lost in thought.

She asked, "How about you? What have you been doing these last few years?"

"Oh, you know me, still drifting from job to job."

"Are you happy?"

Buck thought for a moment, smiled, and said, "Actually, yes. I've gotten to experience many things, see many beautiful places, meet a lot of interesting people, and become friends with quite a few." He added, half-jokingly, "I could have done without the people who were trying to kill me though."

They laughed, just like the old times, as they sat in the glow of warm memories.

Buck added, "That doesn't mean I don't sometimes get lonely. I've often thought of you."

Maria teased, "Good thoughts, I hope."

Buck smiled, "Only the best kind."

She returned his smile and said, "I, too, have often thought of you. Fondly."

# Chapter 7

# Turning the Tables

Buck asked, "What kind of work does Jake do?"

"He's a carpenter. He came to town about two years ago looking for work. The only local construction company was owned by Duff Scroggins. Jake asked around about him and learned he was widely disliked and disrespected. Scroggins treated his employees poorly, paid them next to nothing, and cheated them whenever he could. His customers complained that he charged too much, did sloppy work with inferior materials, was nearly always way behind schedule, and then tried to weasel them out of more money than the quoted price of the job."

Buck said, "Sounds like a varmint badly in need of someone clouding up and raining all over him."

She nodded, and said, "Jake agreed, and saw an opportunity. He started his own construction company, charged fair prices, used good materials, treated his employees and customers fairly, and finished his jobs on schedule."

"I'll bet he got all the business he could handle."

"At first, yes. He won bids for the new schoolhouse, jail, church, and courthouse. Duff Scroggins was furious. He threatened my husband, but Jake didn't back down. Then, one day the only supplier for many miles around started missing deliveries to Jake, supposedly running out of critical materials at the worst possible moment and providing inferior materials at inflated prices to him."

Buck said, "I smell a skunk."

"Jake did, too. He asked around and learned that Duff Scroggins had bribed the supplier, a snake named Bernal Spivey, to do those things to drive Jake out of business. Like Scroggins, Spivey's the only local supplier for what he sells, and he uses that monopoly to gouge his customers. Folks can, of course, buy goods from other companies that are further away, but they have to pay the extra shipping costs when they do and wait longer for the goods. Spivey's no fool: he charges prices that are what they'd have to pay including the freight costs. He wins because he can often give the goods to the customers right away. He and Scroggins have hurt everyone around, one way or another, and stifled the town's growth, but there's no law against what they're doing."

Buck nodded and said, "Just because something isn't illegal doesn't mean a person shouldn't be horsewhipped for doing it."

"Yes, but together they've got this town wrapped up tighter than bark on a tree. Jake's business and reputation have been hurt. To make matters worse, Scroggins started paying wages that are way higher than the jobs are worth and that Jake can afford to pay and making bids that are just low enough that, even if Jake wins the bid, he'll lose a lot of money on the project."

Buck said, "Scroggins must figure that those temporary extra costs are worth it if it quickly drives his only competition out of business."

She sighed, "And it's working. Jake's cornered. He even mortgaged our house to buy more time, but we can't hold out much longer."

After several moments of silence, Buck said, "I have some ideas that might help. I can't promise anything, but I'll try.

Tell Jake that I'll need some time, but if he can hold out for one more month—"

"Oh, Buck! Thank you. That gives us hope. We'll find a way to hold on until we hear back from you."

"Well, I better saddle up and be on my way."

He kissed her on the cheek, thanked her for her hospitality, and hurried toward Buddy.

℘ • ℃

Three weeks later, as Jake walked past the Spivey's Supplies building, he saw a sign reading:

### Under New Management
### Floyd Hawley, Proprietor

Curious, Jake walked inside and was greeted by a man with a medium build and friendly face, who extended his hand and said, "Welcome! I'm the new owner, Floyd Hawley. How may I be of service?"

Jake shook his hand, noticing the firm grip of a man who worked with his hands, and said, "I'm Jake Duncan. Welcome to town."

"Ah, so you're the Jake Duncan that I've heard so much about. I'm honored to meet you and pleased to offer you whatever you need on credit with six months to pay for the first year—and you won't be charged any interest during that time."

"Did I hear you right? You're offering me, a complete stranger, such amazing terms? Don't get me wrong—I'm extremely grateful and all—but I have to ask, why?"

"There are several reasons, actually. The first is that it makes good business sense to help the only honest contractor in town to reestablish himself. Secondly, it's good for my business to help the town grow and prosper. Thirdly, my new business partner speaks highly of you and made the terms a condition of our agreement."

"Your new business partner wouldn't happen to be named Buck Evans, would he?"

Hawley laughed and said, "None other."

Jake joined in the laughter, and said, "In that case, I accept your generous terms. I have a feeling we're going to be doing a lot of business together."

Buck and Maria were sitting on the porch talking when Jake came home. His face lit up when he saw Buck. Duncan bounded up the two porch steps and rushed to shake his hand. "It's great to see you, Buck!"

"Likewise, friend!"

"I just came back from meeting Floyd Hawley. He's a breath of fresh air! How'd you do it?" Duncan sat next to his wife on the porch swing. They clasped hands as Buck explained.

"Well, it was fairly simple, actually. I'm the silent partner in some businesses that manufacture and distribute many of the items that Bernal Spivey buys. When I explained to them the kind of man he was, they told me they had no interest in continuing to do business with him. When they contacted Spivey to tell him they wouldn't do further business with him, they made sure to mention that they would soon be doing business with someone with deep pockets who, due to the customer's higher purchasing volumes, could buy products less expensively than Spivey could. They told him that the man planned to set up shop in this town, and they said that with the man's many advantages, combined with his excellent reputation and Spivey's terrible one, they didn't think that Spivey would be able to stay in business against him for long.

"While Spivey ruminated on the implications of that, I asked my business partners if they knew of anyone whom they'd highly recommend for me to consider as a partner, someone who knew the construction supply and hardware business. Floyd Hawley's name kept coming up. He was a manager of such a company. I went to see him, liked what I saw, and offered him the chance to have his own business with me as his silent partner. He talked to some of my partners about me, and then Floyd and I came to terms.

"By then, Spivey'd had time to stew in his own juices and was panicking. Floyd introduced himself to Spivey, told him what he planned, and made him a buyout offer. Spivey rejected it, demanding more. Floyd held firm and, three days later, bought the business with cash at the originally offered price, but only on the condition that Spivey clear out that night and not return."

ഇ•ൽ

Duff Scroggins soon learned the news. He stormed through Hawley's door and confronted him, "Where's Spivey?"

Hawley's voice chilled a bit at being spoken to so abruptly, but he kept a tone of friendliness in it as he explained, "Spivey sold the business to me. I'm Floyd Hawley. And who might you be?"

In a puffed-up tone, Scroggins said, "I'm your biggest customer. Name's Duff Scroggins."

On hearing the name and in response to the belligerent tone, Hawley said, "Ah, yes, I've heard about you and how you do business, and, frankly, have no desire to do business with you."

Scroggins' face contorted in purple rage, sending specks of spittle flying as he said, "You'll pay for this!"

Hawley leaned into the enraged man's his face and said in a calm tone, "Perhaps, but if I do, I assure you the cost will be far more painful to you than to me. Now get out before I throw you out. And don't come back."

With that, Scroggins turned tail and stormed out, slamming the door behind him.

ഇ•ൽ

The following evening as Hawley closed and began to lock the door to his business, four men appeared from the shadows. Bandanas covered their faces.

One of the men shouted, "Open up, let us in!"

Hawley opened the door and the thugs shoved him inside. The same voice commanded, "Lock the door."

The proprietor did as he was told and said, "Hello, Spivey. I recognize your whiny voice. No sense trying to hide your ugly face. Figured you'd soon be along with some thugs to do your dirty work for you. Four on one is 'bout what I expected from a worm like you." He looked the four over with contempt and said, "You didn't bring enough men."

Spivey said, "Save yer words for coolin' yer soup. I'm gonna love every minute watching them beat you unconscious and torch the place with you in it." He nodded to his thugs to begin.

Hawley leaped, trying to get in position with his back against the front wall so they couldn't get behind and surround him. He blocked two blows, but one of the thugs landed a fist into his gut.

"Oof!" Hawley doubled over.

His assailants didn't see hear the men come out of the back room until it was too late. It cost one thug a punch to the kidney from behind. The man next to him turned and had his nose smashed in. Spivey and the third thug came at them, throwing punches. Buck easily dodged the whiny-voiced worm and landed a hook into the side of the man's head, sending him crashing into a display table full of tools. The third thug threw the classic one-two jab-and-cross combination. The carpenter blocked the jab, but the cross landed hard on his solid right shoulder. Duncan staggered back a step, drawing his opponent in, then returned the favor with an uppercut that jerked the man's chin upward and lifted him onto his toes. He immediately followed with a cross into the thug's neck, folding him like a paper doll.

As Floyd and Jake finished off the thugs, Spivey pulled a knife from his pocket and leaped up. Buck saw the motion from the corner of his eye and turned just in time to catch the full force of the knife thrust into his gut.

Later that evening, Jake and Floyd told Maria what had happened. Jake said, "And then Spivey stabbed Buck."

The loner corrected him, "Actually, he tried to stab me. Once again, Maria saved me."

Maria asked incredulously, "A *third* time? How'd I do it this time?"

Buck pulled his shirt out of his torn pants and showed the jagged hole made by the knife into the front of his left hidden pocket, then pulled a cloth from it that also had a jagged rip in it. Buck opened the folded cloth and two silver dollars clanged onto the table. Buck continued, "The blade sliced through my pants and into the hidden pocket and the cloth inside it and smashed into these coins you gave me for luck when you gave me the shirts and derringer years ago."

They all laughed. Floyd spoke, "If you don't mind my saying so, you're a lucky, lucky man."

Buck said, "With friends like you three, I am indeed."

Maria said, "But what about Spivey and his thugs?"

Jake said, "We unmasked them and I recognized all three. We gave Floyd the choice of what to do with them."

Floyd said, "I could have had them arrested. They would have probably gotten jail time and likely been let out before long. I didn't want such people hanging around town, and there was always a chance that one or more of them would hold a grudge, so I offered them the choice to either be arrested with three witnesses to testify against them or to immediately clear out of town and not come back. They left like their tails were on fire!"

They laughed at the image.

Maria asked, "And Spivey?"

Floyd said, "Well attempted murder is an altogether different matter. We turned him over to the marshal. He said with the evidence and our sworn statements and testimony, Spivey will most likely be convicted of three counts of assault and battery, kidnapping, attempted murder, conspiracy to commit murder, and conspiracy to commit arson. It won't help his case that everyone in town—with the possible exception of Duff Scroggins— despises the man."

They all nodded. Jake said, "It appears that it's going to be a long time before Spivey's going to be in a position to do anything but be prison roped and branded for a long time."

After Hawley head for home that evening and Little Buck was asleep in his cradle, Buck asked, "Have you given any thought to adding a silent partner?"

The couple gave each other a knowing look, and Jake said, "Funny you should ask, because we've already discussed it and were hoping you'd bring it up."

# The End

# About the Author

Best-selling author Russ Towne lives with his wife in Campbell, California USA. They've been married since 1979 and have three adult children and five grandchildren. His passions include spending time with family and friends, writing and publishing in a wide variety of genres, and managing the investments of clients of the wealth management firm he founded in 2003.

**Amazon Author's Page:**
https://www.amazon.com/author/russtowne

**Facebook:**
https://www.facebook.com/russtownebooks/

# Other Books by Russ Towne:

## Westerns

*Western Justice*

*Triggers of Fury*

*Hot Pursuit* (Box Set of the 3 Patch Books)

*Fever*

*A Fighting Chance:*
*Patch Elkins and Gus Roundtree Book Three*

*Last Men Standing:*
*Patch Elkins and Gus Roundtree Book Two*

*Wolverine McLean*

*Six Shots Each Gun*
co-written with Holly Bargo

*Patch: United States Marshal Wanted Dead*

*When All Hell Breaks Loose*

*The Epic Adventures of Longshot Hanson*

*Bordello Justice*

*The Grizzly Creek Massacre*

*Bloody Showdown on Three Falls Creek*

*A Bullet in the Neck*

*A Bloody Day in Destiny*

# Western Romances

*Treasures of the Heart*

*Longshots of the Heart*

# Non-Western Fiction

*Desperate Journeys*
Five suspenseful, action-filled crime stories

*Touched*
Short stories and flash fiction

*Palpable Imaginings*
An anthology of stories by several writers in various genres.

# Nonfiction

*Honest, Honey, That's How It Happened*

*Stop Peeing in the Kitty Litter!*

*Slices of Life*
An anthology of the selected nonfiction
stories of several writers.

*Reflections from the Heart of a Grateful Man*

# Books for Young Children

*Wilbur and the Not-So-Impossible Dream:*
*Book 3 of The Duck Who Flew Upside Down Series*

*The Ducks Who Flew Every Which Way:*
*Book 2 of The Duck Who Flew Upside Down series*

*The Ducks Who Flew Every Which Way:*
*Book 4 of Russ Towne's Children's Stories, (Audiobook)*

*The Duck Who Flew Upside Down and Three More Tales:*
*Book 3 of Russ Towne's Children's Stories (Audiobook)*

*Dragons and Unicorns: Three Magical Tales:*
*Book 2 Russ Towne's Children's Stories (Audiobook)*

*Clyde and Friends:*
*Book 1 Russ Towne's Children's Stories (Audiobook)*

*Sunny Saves the Day*

*Flora Belle and Dreami Dragon*

*Sir Alex Sleighs a Dragon*

*Mysti Z's Magical Day*

*The Beach That Love Built*

*V. G. and Dexter Dufflebee*

*Ki-Gra's Really, Really Big Day*

*The Duck Who Flew Upside Down*

*Zach and the Toad Who Rode a Bull*

*Clyde and Hoozy Whatzadingle*

*Clyde and Friends*

*Clyde and I Help a Hippo to Fly*

*Rusty Bear and Thomas, Too*

*Clyde and I*